Song of the River

GILL LEWIS

Illustrated by
Zanna Goldhawk

Barrington Stoke

First published in 2022 in Great Britain by
Barrington Stoke Ltd
18 Walker Street, Edinburgh, EH3 7LP

www.barringtonstoke.co.uk

A CIP catalogue record for this book is available
from the British Library upon request

ISBN: 978-1-80090-061-5

Printed by Hussar Books, Poland

For Chris Jones, aka the Kernow Beaver,
and for all farmers who protect our future
by giving space for the wild things

Song of the River

Sometimes I feel like a river.

Sometimes I feel like I'm drowning in its sound.

The river rages deep inside of me

and I can't make it stop.

How can you stop a river?

How can you change its song?

CHAPTER 1

I never wanted to live here.

Before we moved to this valley, we lived in the city. Mum, Dad and me.

We lived in a warm flat at the top of a big building. The street was lined with trees and my bedroom overlooked the park. I walked to school every day and at weekends I played with friends.

Every Friday night, Dad and I got fish and chips from the chippy. We all sat in front of the telly eating them from the paper bags with loads of salt and vinegar.

Life was safe. I thought nothing could harm us. There was no warning that life would change. None at all.

But it did.

Dad was knocked off his bike by a lorry. He was in hospital for a long time, and then he died. And I couldn't do anything to stop it.

Dad dying felt like a hurricane sweeping through our lives, taking everything away. It left me and Mum holding on to each other among the wreckage. We knew nothing could be the same again.

Mum said she couldn't live in the city any more. She wanted to get away. She said she wanted to build us a new life. She said life was short and you had to follow your dreams.

She fell in love with a cottage and its garden. I remember her showing me the advert. "It's beautiful, isn't it, Cari?" Mum said to me.

I looked at the white cottage with its garden by a river. It was tucked into a valley at the edge of a small village, hills rising above it. It seemed a world away from our flat in the city.

"Can you imagine it?" said Mum. "We'll make the cottage our own riverside cafe. We'll have tables with red checked tablecloths, plates of carrot cake and flapjacks. There will be spotted teapots and teacups and scones with small pots of cream and jam."

She smiled as she thought about it. "We'll have customers sitting and chatting under the willow trees that line the riverbank. We can do it together. You and me."

And I remember looking at the advert –
at the grassy lawn and the big old trees that
dipped their branches into the sparkling river.
But I couldn't see us being there somehow,
because I knew Dad couldn't be there with
us too.

But Mum bought the cottage. She sold our
flat in the city and we moved in here three
weeks ago, before the end of the summer term.
I left all my friends and school behind.

But the cafe is Mum's dream. Not mine.

I didn't want to leave our old flat at all.

Because leaving the city meant leaving Dad
behind too.

CHAPTER 2

"Cari!" Mum calls to me from downstairs. "Hurry up! I need some help down here."

This is the day of the grand opening of Mum's cafe. Mum planned everything before we even moved into the cottage. She bought and painted old tables and chairs in bright colours. She sewed hems onto checked tablecloths and bought vintage teacups and saucers from charity shops. It means that we are ready to open our doors just three weeks after moving in.

The rich scent of sweet baking and roast coffee swirls up the stairs.

Up here, there's a bedroom each for Mum and me, plus a big room we use as a living room, with a saggy sofa and a TV. The downstairs of our house has become the cafe rooms and kitchen. The cafe spreads out into the long strip of garden that runs alongside the river.

"Cari!" Mum shouts again. "We're opening in fifteen minutes."

I pull on the red-and-white-checked apron that Mum made me. She even said she'd pay me proper money to be a waitress in the cafe. But somehow each new thing we do takes us further and further from Dad. I stop and run my fingers along the chest at the foot of Mum's bed. All of Dad's stuff is in there. All his stuff that Mum didn't want to sell or give away.

I open it and look in, knowing what I'll see. There's all his camera equipment: camera, long lenses and tripods.

Dad was a photographer. He did portraits, weddings and other events. I remember him telling me he loved taking photos because looking through the lens gave you a window into other people's lives. Dad said it gave you a different way to see the world. Underneath the camera gear is Dad's big red woollen jumper he always wore.

I lift the jumper up and bury my nose in it. It still smells of Dad. And my heart aches so deep inside because Dad's jumper is here, but he's not. He can never be here. I can't even see Dad's face. If I try to imagine him, I see him at the hospital. But that's not the dad I know. I just want to go back to our old flat, curl up on the sofa with him and eat fish and chips from the paper. I don't want to be here at all.

"Cari!" Mum says. "Come down! I can see people walking up the lane."

I go downstairs and pick up my notepad and pencil to take the orders. It's a nice day. The sun is shining and the tables in the garden are ready for our customers. Mum's put the tables by the river in the shade of the trees. She's put birdfeeders out too, but I don't think it's such a good idea. I can already see bird droppings on the clean tablecloths and I'm sure I saw a rat swimming in the river the other day.

The river looks almost pretty today in the sunlight. Mum says she loves hearing the sound of the water. She says it makes her feel calm. But I can see there's a power to the river. I can hear its angry rumble as it surges down the valley. It's dark and churning under its sparkling surface. I feel angry like the river too.

I look along the lane and see a family walking towards us: a mum, a dad and a boy

and girl. The girl looks about my age. I step
back into the kitchen. It feels as if Mum and I
are half a family now. Suddenly I don't want to
be seen.

"Come on, Cari," says Mum. "I need your
help." She pulls a batch of freshly baked
brownies from the oven.

I force a sparkling smile and walk out into
the garden where the family have sat down at
a table.

"You must be Cari," says the woman.

I nod.

"I met your mum in the post office
yesterday," she goes on, smiling. "I'm Mandy,
and this is my husband, Alan. And this is
Emmi and Ollie."

Ollie's younger than his sister. He's sliding in his seat, fidgeting as if he doesn't want to be here.

Mum comes out and joins in the chat. "Hello again," she says to Mandy. Mum turns to me. "These are our neighbours, Cari."

Mandy nods and says, "We're from Beverley Farm up the valley."

Mum then turns to Emmi. "Cari will be in your class at school after the summer. That'll be nice, won't it, Cari?"

I smile, but I want to shrink away. I've always been shy. I'm never sure how other people know what to say. And I don't want to go to the school here. I want to be back at my old school with my old friends.

Emmi smiles but says nothing too.

"What can we get you?" asks Mum. "Tea? Coffee? Cakes?"

I take the order back to the kitchen with Mum and already there are other people sitting down at the tables.

We're busy all morning and into the afternoon. It's not until 5 p.m. that we finally stop serving and put the closed sign on the gate.

We're clearing up when a young man and woman cycle up to the gate. They look out of breath.

"Are we too late?" asks the man.

I can see Mum doesn't want to say no. "We're shut now, but I could get you a cup of tea and piece of hummingbird cake," she says. "It's all we've got left today."

"Perfect," says the woman. "Thank you."

They take a seat by the river. I make the tea and put two pieces of cake on plates and take it to them.

By the time I get there, the woman is crouching down on her knees and looking past the long grasses to the river.

She turns to the man and asks, "Luke, did you see it?"

Luke shakes his head.

"There!" she says. "It's on the other side."

I look across and see a rat swimming in the water, its nose above the surface.

"Oh yes!" said Luke. "You're right, Jenny. A water vole. I'm surprised it's here. They normally like slow-flowing water."

"It's not a rat?" I say.

They both turn and Jenny smiles. "No," she replies. "It's a water vole. They're very rare. Luke and I work at the nature reserve above Beverley Farm and we've been trying to attract water voles for years. I didn't know they were here."

I shrug. It's small and brown and looks like a rat to me. I can't see why they are so excited about it.

"And these are common blue damselflies," says Jenny. She points at what look like blue dragonflies rising up in front of her.

Luke sees me frowning and laughs. "Watch out," he says. "If you spend any time round Jenny, she'll turn you into a wildlife fanatic too."

I put the hummingbird cake down and walk back into the house.

I don't want to be turned into a wildlife fanatic.

I don't want to have to make new friends.

I want to be back home with my old friends.

I want everything to go back to how it was before.

And I hate Mum for taking all those things away from me.

CHAPTER 3

The cafe is busy all summer.

Really busy.

We have lots of regular customers from the village and many tourists too.

A knitting group meets here every Monday. Jenny and Luke come every day on their way up to the nature reserve. Jenny always stops to look at the water voles. Mandy from Beverley Farm comes for a meet-up with her farmer friends. She invited me to Emmi's birthday party, but I felt too shy to go. Emmi and her

friends would all know each other and I'd just be in the way. I wouldn't know who to talk to.

But Mum chats to everyone. And I see her smiling.

She looks happy, but I don't want her to be this happy. How can she be happy when we've lost Dad? Maybe she's so busy with everything here that she's even forgetting him.

Mum is up really early every morning, making cakes and biscuits for the day ahead. Then after the cafe has closed, she cleans up and gets ready for the next day. In the evening, she's so tired that she falls asleep in front of the TV.

Mum doesn't have any time for me.

My old friends don't have time for me either. They don't call me so much any more,

and when they do, they tell me about the parties and trips that I've missed.

It feels as if everyone's life is moving on and I'm the one left behind.

I just want to go back home. I want my bed in my bedroom that overlooks the city park. I want my old life back. I want my friends. And I want my dad.

And now it's got to the end of the summer holidays and it's the first day of school tomorrow. I don't want to go and I feel sick inside thinking about it. I'll be going into Year Six at the village school. Everyone will know each other. They'll have known each other for years. They won't want a new person in their class. They won't want me.

The fields look dry and brown after the long hot summer. The leaves on the trees are

starting to turn yellow and there is the smell of autumn in the air. Even time is moving on, pulling us away from Dad.

I stand behind the counter in the cafe and close my eyes and wish for something to take me away from here.

As if in response, a grumpy wind snatches the fallen leaves and whips them around.

The weather seems to match my mood. The clouds get darker and darker and lower and lower, covering the hills. It feels as if the whole sky is pressing down on us.

It must be raining up on the hills already because the river has risen higher. It sounds even angrier than normal. The dark water is flecked with white as it churns past our garden.

I shut the windows to block out the sound, but I can still feel the river churning deep inside of me too.

A sudden gust of wind flips some of the chairs and whips the tablecloths across the garden.

"Help me get these chairs in," shouts Mum.

I run and help her fold up the chairs and bring them inside the house.

Mum looks out at the dark sky. "The forecast says there's a storm coming."

I hear a note of worry in her voice as she says, "We'll close the cafe early today."

At that moment rain begins to fall. Big fat heavy raindrops make black spots on the dry patio.

The nearest willow tree creaks and groans in the wind. The river pulls at its branches that trail in the water.

I wished so hard to go back to my old home in the city, to get away from here. But not even I would have wished for the storm that was coming.

CHAPTER 4

The sky is so dark that it feels like evening when it's only late afternoon. There's nothing much to do, so I get changed into my pyjamas and pull on my dressing gown. I go down to the kitchen and find Mum standing by the window, looking out into the garden.

I go over and lean into her, and she puts her arm around me.

The rain is coming down harder now, the raindrops bouncing on the patio and path. The kitchen window is smeared with rain and everything looks misshapen through the glass. Wide puddles are spreading across the garden.

It's hard to imagine people sitting there in summer sunlight.

Rain is drumming on the cottage roof, but there's another sound that rises above that – a deep roar that seems to fill the house. The river. The water has risen even higher and almost reaches the top of the riverbank.

"Do you think it'll flood?" I ask.

Mum says nothing at first, but her arm holds me closer. "I'm sure the rain will stop soon," she says.

The sky grows even darker and the garden is lost in rain and shadow. It seems scary.

Mum takes a step back from the window. Maybe she feels the same way too.

"Come on," says Mum. "Let's go upstairs and watch a movie. I've got popcorn somewhere and we can have ice cream."

Mum and I curl up on the sofa and watch Disney films. It's a long time since we've done this together, but I don't think we're really watching. We're both listening to the river.

It sounds wild and angry.

Then there's a moment of silence and suddenly it sounds like the gurgle of water is right next to us.

I jump up to look first.

"Mum!" I yell. The river has burst its banks and is now right outside our house.

Mum joins me. We can't see our garden any more. All we can see is rushing water.

Lots and lots of rushing water.

Our car alarm starts shrieking.

Mum runs to the bathroom window to look out of the other side of the house. "The car!" she cries. "The river's taking it away."

We're surrounded by the river.

"It's coming in the house!" shouts Mum.

She flies down the stairs and starts bringing up books and bags and anything she can carry. I hear her sloshing through the water.

"Stay up there," Mum says. "I'll pass things to you."

She grabs whatever she can from the cafe – crockery and cutlery, menus and

tablecloths – and I take them and carry them into our bedrooms, but the speed of the flood scares me. The black water keeps rising and rising up the stairs – onto the first step, then the second, then the third.

A sudden electric blue spark lights up the house and crackles across the water.

Then all the lights go out.

Mum screams.

"Mum!" I yell.

"Stay out of the water," shouts Mum.

It's pitch-black, but I hear her climbing the stairs. She grabs me and holds me tightly. "The river's coming right through the house," Mum says.

"We need to phone the fire brigade," I say.

Mum reaches into her pocket. "I've left my phone downstairs."

"We can use the landline," I say.

"The power is off," says Mum. "The phone won't work. We're stuck. There's nothing we can do. It's too dangerous to go outside."

And so Mum and I cling to each other in the darkness, listening to the wild roar of the black water rising up the stairs towards us.

CHAPTER 5

Last night seemed to last for ever. The flood swirled up to the eighth step. We could hear chairs floating in the rooms downstairs, clunking into the walls and ceilings. I thought it would rise up into our bedrooms, but finally the rain stopped and the flood water started to slowly sink back down the stairs.

We don't go to bed until it starts getting light outside. Mum and I crawl into her bed and wrap the duvet around us.

I don't think I'll be able to sleep at all, but I do. I fall into a deep and dreamless sleep.

When I wake up, morning light is shining through the window. I'm alone in Mum's bed.

There's a strange stillness and silence.

I look out of the window and see the river has retreated to its banks, but it has washed our garden tables away. The flower beds are just bare soil.

I go down the stairs and stand on the bottom step. The ground floor is covered in thick, stinky mud.

Mum is in welly boots, trying to sweep the mud outside, but there's so much that it doesn't seem to make any difference. I hope she doesn't make me go to school today.

Mum stops sweeping and throws the broom to the ground. Then she sits down on a chair, puts her head in her hands and sobs. Mum sobs

and sobs. I've never really heard her cry like this, even after Dad died.

"Mum?" I say.

She turns and sees me watching. "Oh, Cari, we've lost everything."

I've never seen Mum look more lost than she does now.

"We'll be OK, won't we?" I ask.

Mum shakes her head. "I thought I could make this work, but I can't. I'm sorry, Cari."

Hot tears burn in my eyes. I feel anger rising inside. Fear too. "I never even wanted to come here," I shout at her.

"I know," says Mum. "It was a stupid idea."

My heart is thumping in my chest. "What are we going to do?" I ask.

Mum holds out her arms like she wants to hold me. "Come here."

But I don't go to her. It feels as if the river is still raging inside me, tumbling and churning. "This is all your fault," I tell her, and I back away up the stairs.

I don't want Mum. I want Dad. I want Dad to hug me and tell me everything will be all right.

I open the chest and take out Dad's thick red jumper. I pull it on. It's much too big, but it wraps me in a huge hug as if his arms are around me. I can still smell him in the jumper.

I lift up Dad's camera. It feels heavy in my hands. Real. It's one of those expensive

cameras with lots of dials and buttons. Dad
said it made photography look complicated,
but all you really need to know is how much
light to let in. He taught me how to photograph
birds in flight so you can see each feather of
the wing. He explained how to take a portrait
of someone so that they are in sharp focus
but the background is a bit blurry. I miss him
teaching me. I hold the viewfinder to my eye
and look through.

Maybe this is like looking through Dad's
eyes at the world. Maybe if I use his camera, I
can somehow bring Dad back here too.

Maybe Dad can help us.

I walk quietly back downstairs. Mum
doesn't see me at first. She's still sitting on
the chair looking out of the window. I hold the
camera to my eye and look through. The soft
light in the room catches one side of Mum's

face, leaving the other in deep shadow. She looks so sad.

I keep looking through the lens and begin to see her as a person, not just as Mum. She looks broken somehow.

And suddenly I realise that I'm not angry at her. I'm angry at everything that's happened.

Mum is hurting just as much as me.

I press the shutter – click.

Mum looks round. At first, she does a double-take at me with Dad's jumper and his camera. Then she says, "Leave me alone, Cari. Don't take pictures of me. Not like this."

I pull on my welly boots and head outside. The sun is now shining and the air is sharp but clear and bright. I hold the camera to my eye,

trying to see what Dad would have seen, trying to make sense of all this.

I look at the river that has returned to the riverbank. It's still fast and furious, spilling over the rocks and swirling through the valley. I change the settings of the camera to slow shutter speed like Dad showed me. I take the photo and see the raging river as a blur of white. Then I change the setting to a fast shutter speed and capture a split second, a tiny moment of time. I can see a droplet of water suspended in mid-air. I feel like that droplet of water. Suspended. Waiting to fall.

I kneel down on the muddy grass and take photo after photo. I see the tiny raindrops on the ends of willow leaves. Close up they look like tiny beads of light. Moss on a stone looks like a forest. The world is still beautiful even after this storm. Then I see the water vole. It's

swimming along the river and hops out onto the side and begins chewing grasses.

I look through the viewfinder and let the vole fill the screen. Its eyes are small and bright, and its cheeks move fast, chewing on the grass. It keeps turning its head from side to side and then plops into the river again where it starts digging out soil from its flooded burrow.

Another vole appears and they both scrape out soil that's flooded into their hole. They work together and don't stop until the hole into their burrow is clear. It's almost like Dad's showing me that if the water voles can clear up and survive after the storm, then so can we.

I'm so absorbed in watching them that I don't hear the gate open and close.

Jenny and Luke have arrived.

"Hey, we came to see how you guys are doing after the storm," says Luke. "The village has been badly hit. The library was flooded, and the pub car park is full of water."

I stand up and turn to them. "We lost everything too," I say.

"Oh no," says Jenny. She looks around. "Is your mum in?"

They follow me into the kitchen, where Mum is still sitting on the chair.

"Sorry about the flood," says Luke. "Jenny and I can help clear up."

"Yes," Jenny says, smiling. "We need to help you get the cafe open again so we can enjoy your delicious cakes."

Mum shakes her head. "I shouldn't have bought this place. We can't open ever again."

"We can," I say. "The water voles are back in their burrows. If they can do it, so can we."

"Water voles?" says Mum. She looks irritated, as if water voles are the last thing on her mind.

I nod and show everyone the photos I took.

"These are great photos," says Luke.

"I can't do it," Mum interrupts. "I haven't got the money to pay for the flood damage."

"Won't the insurance pay?" asks Luke.

Mum puts her head in her hands. "I couldn't get flood insurance. It was stupid of me to buy this place. Even if we do clear up this time,

there'll be another storm and another flood.
We'll lose everything again. There's nothing
I can do to stop the river. There's nothing
anyone can do to stop the river."

"Actually, there is," says Jenny.

I look at her. "What do you mean?" I ask.

"We know something that can stop the
flooding," says Jenny. "But we'll need your help
to make it happen."

CHAPTER 6

"Beavers," says Jenny.

"Beavers?" I say.

Jenny nods. She pulls her iPad from her bag and taps on the screen. There's a picture of a beaver. It looks a bit like a giant guinea pig with a leathery tail in the shape of a paddle and a pair of huge orange front teeth.

"Beavers were hunted in Britain hundreds of years ago and became extinct," says Jenny. "But we really need them back now."

"Beavers can change rivers," says Luke. "People often try to make rivers straight and remove fallen trees and other blockages. This makes water rush down a river really fast. It means if there's a sudden downpour the river can flood. But beavers cut down trees with their massive teeth and make dams."

Mum stares at the picture of the beaver. "I can't see how beavers can make that much difference," she says. "How can they stop all that water running from the hills?"

"Beavers create pools and wetlands," says Jenny. "They can slow rivers. So if there's a sudden storm, the water is released much more slowly downstream."

"They're great for other wildlife too," says Luke. "More wetlands mean more plants, more insects and more frogs and toads and birds."

"So why do you need our help?" I ask.

"Not everyone here wants beavers," says Jenny. "We're having a difficult time convincing the community to agree to have beavers on the nature reserve. Please come to the village hall tomorrow if you can. We need some support. We need to make the local council realise that it's a good idea to introduce the beavers."

"You really think they can stop the flooding?" I ask.

Jenny nods. "I know so," she says. "I've seen it happen in other countries. I've studied these creatures for a long time."

I want to ask more questions, but two firemen turn up to check the electrics are safe.

I say goodbye to Jenny and Luke, but my head is swirling. If we can bring the beavers to this valley, then maybe we can save our cafe too.

The firemen tell us that the electrics in the house are damaged and unsafe. They say we'll have to get an electrician to fix the mess and live somewhere else in the village until it's safe to come back.

Mum shakes her head. "I don't have the money, Cari. I'll have to borrow more from the bank. If we can't pay it back, we'll lose this house. We'll lose everything."

"What else can we do?" I say.

Mum holds me close and puts her head on mine. "I'm sorry, Cari. I thought I could build a new life for us, but I can't. I got it wrong."

And as we stand there, I know we can't go back to the city again. Dad isn't there any more. It can never be the same. But now Mum's so sad. She's giving up on her dream and I'm scared I'm losing her now too.

"We'll be OK, Mum," I say.

I go upstairs and look again at the photo I took of Mum looking out of the window in the light and shade. I see her as Dad might have seen her, and I know Dad wouldn't want her to give up on her dreams. If beavers are the answer to saving Mum's dream, then I have to make sure the beavers come back. I have to do it for Dad. I have to make this work for all of us.

I have to be brave.

There can be no going back. Only forwards.

I have to make our life here, in this valley.

I change into my new school uniform, grab my bag and go downstairs.

Mum looks at me and frowns. "Where are you going?" she asks.

I force myself to smile. "I'm a bit late for the first day, but I don't think they'll mind." I take a deep breath. "I'm on my way to school."

CHAPTER 7

Sometimes you can worry about something so much that it grows into a huge problem in your head. The fear of it becomes worse than the thing itself. School was like that. I'd dreaded it so much over the summer that I'd felt sick at the thought of it. But I actually enjoyed my first day.

The school is really tiny and sits on a hill overlooking the valley. It's so small that Years Five and Six are together in one class. Emmi and the three other girls in the class are really friendly. The teacher, Miss Williams, is really nice too.

Of course, everyone was talking about last night's flood, including Alfie, a boy in my class. Alfie's mum and dad own the pub in the village, and he was telling us how all the car alarms were going off as the flood filled the car park. His dad even had to wade through the deep water to rescue their cat. Hearing other people's stories made me feel brave enough to tell everyone that we'd been flooded too.

Miss Williams finally got everyone to stop talking about the flood and announced what we'd be doing this term.

"It's World Environmental Health Day later this month," she said. "So we'll be doing projects on the environment. For your homework this week, I want you all to research an animal and make a leaflet to explain how it has adapted to its habitat. And show why we need to protect it."

Alfie shot his hand in the air and asked, "Can we do aliens?"

"Just animals on this planet, please," Miss Williams said. "You can work on your own or with a friend. And hand it in at the end of the week."

I sat with Emmi and her friends at lunch.

"I'm going to do orangutans for my homework," said Emmi. "They're my favourite."

"I'm going to do tigers," said Nikki. "They're really endangered."

"I'm doing gorillas," said Bella. She turned to me. "Have you decided what you'll do?"

I shook my head. "I'm not sure," I said. But I knew exactly what I'd do. An animal much, much closer to home. The beaver.

*

When Alfie told his mum that we didn't have anywhere to live, she said we could have one of the guest rooms at the pub free of charge until our house was OK again. So after my first day at school, Luke and Jenny helped us carry some things from our house as our car got flooded too. Mum says we can't afford another car for a while. Our room in the pub is small and has twin beds, but it's cosy for now.

I leave Mum upstairs and go down into the bar area. Alfie's mum said I can use the tables to work at before the pub opens in the evening. I spread my paper and pens on the table and open my laptop to find out all I can about beavers.

Alfie comes in and stops to look at my homework. "What animal are you doing?" he asks.

"Beavers," I say.

"Beavers!" says Alfie. "Why beavers?"

"They can stop the flooding," I say.

Alfie takes a seat beside me and watches me researching on my laptop. "Can I do it with you?" he asks.

"If you want," I say.

"I don't like writing," says Alfie. "I'll do the drawings. I'm good at drawing."

"Cool," I say. And it is cool. Because I'd almost forgotten how good it feels to have friends.

Alfie does a big drawing of a beaver as I find out all about them. He *is* really good at

drawing. When he's finished, I write the words and information around the picture.

European Beaver
Length: up to 1m including the tail
Weight: 25–30 kg
Lifespan: 7 years
Diet: plants
The world's second biggest rodent.

Beavers cut down trees with their sharp teeth and make dams. They create wetlands for other important wildlife. The dams trap sediment, improving water quality, and reduce the risk of flooding downstream. The rivers become healthier. Healthy rivers mean more fish too.

"We need to write about why beavers went extinct in this country," I say.

Beside me, Alfie looks at the screen. "It says people hunted them for fur."

I read on. "It wasn't just for fur," I say. "It says they release an oil from glands near their bottoms that's used to make perfumes."

"That's gross," says Alfie. "You're kidding, right?"

"Nope," I say. "The oil is called castoreum. It's still put into some perfumes today. It's even used in foods like vanilla ice cream."

"Ugh!" says Alfie. "Beaver bum juice! I'm not eating ice cream again." He takes his pencil and draws an arrow to the beaver's bottom. Alfie writes: *Beaver bum juice – used for perfume and ice cream.*

I find myself laughing out loud and then suddenly realise I haven't laughed like this for a long, long time.

I take another piece of paper. "We need to write about how beavers change rivers," I say.

Alfie looks at the long article on the computer screen. "Can't I draw it?" he says. "I don't want to write it all out."

"How do we draw it?" I say.

"Simple," says Alfie. "We'll draw two landscapes: one without beavers and another with beavers."

"Brilliant!" I say. And it is a brilliant idea. We have to show what a valley with beavers could look like so we can get people to agree that beavers are a good thing.

In the first picture Alfie draws hills and a fast-flowing river and a flooded village. For more impact I add people being washed away too, with their arms in the air calling for help.

In the second picture Alfie draws the same hills, but now with beavers and their dams. He draws ponds and wide pools. I add wildlife, drawing a heron, some toads and dragonflies. I add flowers like marsh marigolds.

Alfie's mum comes into the room. "There you are, Alfie," she says. "You were so quiet I thought you were up to no good."

"We're doing homework," says Alfie.

His mum's eyebrows shoot up with surprise. "Well, I don't want to stop you, but we're opening the bar in fifteen minutes."

"It's OK," I say. "We're almost done."

Alfie's mum smiles. "Would you like to eat some lasagne and chips with Alfie?" she asks me.

"Yes, please," I say.

We're finishing our supper when Mum comes down from our room.

Mum turns to Alfie's mum and says, "You must let me know how much I owe you for Cari's meal."

Alfie's mum smiles. "No need," she says. "Cari can have double helpings if it means Alfie will do his homework."

Mum looks at our drawings. "These are really good," she says. "It's hard to imagine beavers could change the landscape so much."

Alfie's mum looks closely at them too. "Imagine if beavers really could stop the flooding. We've been flooded several times and it's happening more often too."

"Jenny says beavers can stop the flooding," I tell her. "They've been reintroduced into lots of areas already."

"Well, let's hope people vote for them here," says Mum.

Alfie's mum sighs. "There's a lot of people who don't want beavers."

"But why?" I ask. "I don't understand. If they can stop the flooding, why wouldn't anyone want them?"

"Well, I guess we're going to find out tomorrow night," says Mum. "There's the meeting about it in the village hall."

I look at the two pictures we've drawn.

I know which landscape I want to see. It's the only way we can live here. This is our home now, no matter what I felt before. We need to have beavers here again.

And I know we might have to fight for it.

CHAPTER 8

We're some of the first people to arrive at the village hall.

Alfie and his mum and dad sit down beside us.

I'm wearing Dad's red jumper as a lucky charm. It makes me feel like he's here with us too.

Luke and Jenny are already in the hall, trying to get their PowerPoint presentation to work on the screen on stage. Jenny looks nervous, reading and re-reading her notes.

Soon other people begin to trickle in. I turn around and see Emmi's parents from Beverley Farm. Emmi's dad looks grumpy and he sits with his arms folded, staring ahead. There are other farmers I recognise too.

Then a tall red-faced man comes in the room. He walks up and down the front row of seats but can't find a free one. So he takes a seat from the back and puts it in the front row, right in the middle of the aisle.

"That's Rufus Grub," Alfie's mum whispers. "He's on the town council. He's the one who put spikes on the village hall roof to stop birds perching there."

Rufus Grub sits down and clears his throat loudly to get Jenny's attention. "When is this going to start?" Rufus asks. "We don't have all evening."

Jenny looks a bit flustered as she puts the first slide on the screen. It's of the flood waters in the village.

"This village has been flooded six times in ten years," Jenny says. "And we know that with climate change these floods are likely to get worse and more frequent."

I take Mum's hand in mine and hold it tight.

"But we have an answer that could save the village from floods," Jenny says, clicking on to the next slide.

The screen fills with the image of several really cute animals.

"Beavers!" Jenny grins.

There's some muttering in the crowd, but Jenny continues.

"These creatures were once widespread in this country, but they were hunted to extinction. Beavers are really important and are known as a keystone species because they support lots and lots of wildlife. But one of the important things about them for us is that they can change rivers. Beavers can hold back floods. And up at the nature reserve we are planning to release beavers into big enclosures to see what effect they can have."

Jenny shows some other slides and explains how beavers gnaw trees and cut them down. She shows how beavers create dams and big pools that can hold back millions of gallons of water and slow a river.

"But we need your help," says Jenny. "The nature reserve needs funding for the plan and also your approval. So if you want to help

beavers and slow the river, please sign our petition and we can make this happen."

Beside Jenny, Luke adds, "If you have any questions, we are very happy to try to answer them."

Emmi's dad stands up. "I don't want beavers," he says. "They do lots of damage to farmland. They dig into the riverbanks, making them unstable. They flood good pasture and they will eat our crops."

Jenny smiles, but I can see she looks nervous facing Emmi's dad.

"The beavers will be in the fenced enclosure," Jenny says.

"But beavers have escaped in other parts of the country and done lots of damage," says

Emmi's dad. "It would only be a matter of time until they escaped here too."

There's a rumble of agreement from the back of the room.

Then Rufus Grub stands up. He looks down his long nose at Jenny and says, "I don't like the sound of beavers making a mess. There is a silly trend for rewilding – letting nature take over. We must listen to our farmers, as they have been looking after the land for hundreds of years. They are the guardians of the countryside."

Jenny faces Rufus now and replies, "With respect, Mr Grub, beavers were here long before these farmers. And we have to look after the wild. Britain is one of the most nature-depleted countries in the world. We've lost over half our native species in the last fifty

years. We have to do more to bring the wild back."

Mr Grub points a long bony finger at her. "You haven't thought this through, have you?" he says. "I'm a keen fisherman, so you tell me, what about the fish? How do we stop the beavers eating all the fish?"

Jenny's mouth just drops open. But Alfie gets up and turns to Mr Grub. "Beavers don't even eat fish," Alfie says. "Beavers are vegetarian."

There's a ripple of laughter and Mr Grub's face goes an even deeper shade of red. Jenny nods and says, "Beavers' dams and pools are actually good for fish."

But Emmi's dad stands up again. "That may be true," he says. "But if the beavers escape, they'll ruin our farmland and be bad

for business. We can't have them in this valley.
I won't have it."

Another farmer stands up and adds, "I
agree. Fields could become waterlogged due to
beaver activity, which will be a waste of good
farmland. Beavers will damage our land and
take away our livelihoods."

I can feel fear and anger boil up inside
me. If we can't have beavers, then Mum and I
will have to leave here. Maybe this is my only
chance to speak out and save us. I wrap my
arms around Dad's jumper and stand up. But
I'm shaking inside.

I turn to face the farmers. "What about *our*
livelihood?" I say. I feel hot tears running down
my cheeks. "The flood took everything from
Mum and me. If there's another flood, we'll lose
our house for ever. We'll lose our home. I don't
even know where we'll go. All you'll lose is a

little bit of land. What makes your fields more important than my home?"

I sit back down next to Mum and she holds my hand tightly. The hall is silent. But I'm still raging inside.

Jenny stands up again and says, "We'd like to reassure everyone again that the beavers will be in fenced enclosures on the reserve."

Another farmer speaks out. "Well, if they escape, I'm taking my shotgun out."

This time Mum stands up. "Well, you're not exactly a guardian of the countryside then, are you?" she snaps at him. "More like the murderer."

The atmosphere in the room is stormy.

Luke closes the meeting by asking people to sign a petition to persuade the council to agree that the nature reserve can introduce beavers to the valley.

I look at all the other people as we walk out of the hall. Will enough of them sign the petition to bring back the beavers? Have they listened?

I want to know if we've saved our home here. But it's impossible to know what they are thinking.

CHAPTER 9

Mum and I move back into our cottage
in October and Mum re-opens the cafe in
November.

Jenny told us that we won't know if the
petition has been successful until after
New Year.

"I'll wait until then, Cari," Mum says. "But
if the beaver plan doesn't go ahead, I'm putting
the cottage up for sale. We can't risk another
flood. We'll sell up and find somewhere else."

And I feel so sad because I don't want to move from here now. I've got new friends. I want to fight to save our home.

The cafe is slow to get going again. Maybe it's because it's winter and there are fewer tourists. But some of Mum's regular customers haven't returned. Emmi's mum no longer meets her farmer friends here for lunch. Maybe it's because we support the beaver plan. At least Jenny and Luke come in nearly every day.

On the last day of term, Mum almost misses the afternoon when parents can come into school and see all the work we've done. I'm left waiting for her while all the other parents and their children are together.

I see other parents looking at the artwork and displays in the hall. Emmi is showing her mum her project on orangutans. Then her

mum looks at all the other displays and stops at the one Alfie and I did on beavers. She looks at it for a long, long time.

I'm relieved when Mum arrives at last. I pull her in the other direction because I don't want to hear Emmi's mum tell me she doesn't want the beavers.

*

We spend Christmas and New Year in the cottage, just Mum and me. It's our first Christmas without Dad. I can't wait for the holidays to be over, but they seem to drag on much longer than normal.

The winter rains have made the river run even faster, and Mum closes the curtains every evening to shut it out. I don't like its deep roar. She can't bear to look at it or hear it either.

*

The first snowdrops of early spring are pushing up from the ground when Jenny and Luke come to see us.

"Do you want the good news or the bad news?" says Luke.

"The good news," I say.

"Well," says Jenny, "we got enough signatures on the petition in favour of the beavers."

"That's brilliant," I say.

"But," says Luke, "the bad news is that it still has to be approved by the local council, and Mr Grub is a councillor. There's going to be an open meeting next week."

Mum shakes her head and says, "Mr Grub won't want beavers even if they are good for fish. He's one of those people who just can't stand change."

Jenny nods. "There are farmers on the council too."

"Mandy from Beverley Farm is one of the councillors," says Luke. "Beverley Farm is just below the reserve, so people will listen to what she has to say."

"It's not fair," I say. "The beaver plan is never going to be approved now."

*

It's the longest week, waiting for the meeting.

The meeting that will decide if we stay or if we go.

The meeting that will decide if we have to leave our home.

The roar of the river seems to fill my head and run inside me so that I can't think at all.

I don't really want to go to the meeting, but Mum says we have to. We meet Alfie and his mum and dad at the village hall too. The council members are there at a table on the stage. This time no one can ask questions; we can only listen.

Mr Grub stands up and begins, "Yes, many people voted for the beavers, but I say we don't have them back. We haven't had beavers here for hundreds of years and we have managed fine without them. They'll make a mess of the countryside."

Another councillor nods. "And if they escape, they could cause lots of problems."

Then Mandy, Emmi's mum, stands up. "The beavers could certainly damage our land if they escape from the reserve," she says.

I feel my heart drop. Everyone is going to listen to her.

"But ..." Mandy continues, "Mr Grub is wrong. We haven't managed fine without them. Beavers were here long before us. Nature has suffered at our hands. Before Christmas, I went to my daughter's school to see the projects they had been working on. Emmi had done one on orangutans, about saving wild places in Borneo for the creatures who live there and reversing the effects of climate change. But two children from her school had done a project on beavers. They helped me to imagine what this valley could look like with beavers. These creatures can repair the damage we have done. I can't directly help the orangutans, but I *can* help the

beavers. And I want to do it. I want to help them so my daughter can thank me in years to come. In fact, I have just found out that Beverley Farm means *Stream of the Beavers*. So they do belong here after all."

Mandy looks at me as she sits down and gives a little nod.

And suddenly I feel a rush of hope.

The meeting seems to last for ever, but then final votes are taken and a decision is made.

Mr Grub stands up and unfolds a piece of paper.

The room falls silent.

Mr Grub clears his throat and reads. "The council agree," he says, "that beavers can be brought back to the valley."

CHAPTER 10

The beavers arrive on a cold March day with blue skies and bright white clouds. A chilly wind is blowing, tugging on my coat and scarf.

"Can't you come and watch the beavers be released?" I ask Mum.

"I've got lots of table bookings today," says Mum. "It's going to be busy. Besides, I'll watch it on the local news tonight. Jenny said a camera crew are coming."

Mum's right. There's a camera crew at the reserve, plus lots of visitors, our local politician and even Rufus Grub. Jenny asks me to take

some photos for her. She says I have special priority as the official photographer.

The beavers arrive in two big metal boxes. They're named Gracie and Harold, and they already know each other. They are a pair from another reserve.

We all stand back and Jenny opens the hatches of the boxes. It takes a few minutes for the beavers to put their noses outside the boxes. Gracie comes out first, sniffing the air.

I've seen pictures of beavers of course, but they seem even bigger in real life. Their bodies are covered in dense brown fur and they have little front paws they hold in front of them as if they are praying. Their hind legs are chunky and I can see they have webs between their toes. But the most noticeable thing about them is their leathery tails shaped like a paddle.

I start clicking on the camera as Gracie steps onto the grass. She lifts her nose in the air and then sees the river. She waddles across the grass and slides into the water, dipping and diving as if she's lived here her whole life. Harold follows shortly after.

The camera crew interview Jenny and Luke, and then people start to drift away. I want to stay longer, but I promised Mum that I'd help out in the cafe.

When I get back home, the cafe is full. Even the camera crew are here, eating cake. Mum has made a special chocolate log beaver cake that's very popular.

Finally, it's near closing time and there are only a few people left. I'm clearing tables when I see Emmi and her mum and dad coming through the gate.

They take a seat by the river and I go over with my notepad and pencil.

"Cup of tea? Coffee?" I ask.

Mandy smiles and reaches into her bag. "We've brought our own drink," she says. "We hoped you and your mum might join us." Mandy takes out a bottle of sparkling wine and a bottle of lemonade and puts them on the table.

"To welcome the beavers," says Emmi.

Mandy smiles a bigger smile. "And to welcome our neighbours too. We're glad you're staying."

I grin. "I'll just get some glasses," I say. "And I'll get Mum too."

*

All through March and April, I spend a lot of time up at the reserve. I get to know Gracie and Harold well and I can sit for hours just watching them. They're always busy and it's amazing to see how much they have changed their enclosure in just one month.

They have cut down small trees with their sharp teeth. The chewed trunks stick up like sharpened pencils. Some of the trunks have fallen across the main channel of the river, damming back the water.

The beavers have pulled twigs and branches into place to make a big dome that Jenny calls their lodge. It's huge. The beavers swim underwater through tunnels to get to a safe resting space beneath the lodge. There are lots of small pools behind the main dam and lots of wildlife too.

I photograph newts swimming to the surface. A bird called a hobby whizzes by, snatching dragonflies from the air. A heron stands on one leg, searching the dark water for frogs to eat. The whole landscape is changing from a straight river to lots of small pools with little streams pouring from one to another.

But it's not just the landscape and the shape of the river that has changed. I didn't notice it at first, but the sound of the river has changed too. It doesn't sound so fierce and constant as it did before. It burbles and tinkles. It gurgles and splashes. The deep raging undercurrent of the river has gone.

When I mention this to Jenny, she smiles. "The river is learning to sing a different song. People would have heard this over four hundred years ago when there were beavers here before."

"A four-hundred-year-old song!" I say.

"And just wait till we get even more birds," said Jenny. "The cut trees don't die but send up lots of new shoots that create more woodland. Who knows? We might even get nightingales."

"Nightingales?" I ask.

Jenny nods. "They're nothing special to look at, but they have the most beautiful song of all."

I take loads of photos of the beavers swimming, playing, chewing wood and oiling their fur with castoreum to keep their coats waterproof.

I think the beavers have got used to me being there, because they don't seem to mind me and even come pretty close. The way they hold things in their front paws makes them

look like tiny hands. And their big leathery
paddle tails help them swim through the water.

*

But in the last week of April I begin to get
worried. I haven't seen Gracie for a while.
What if she has escaped into the surrounding
farmland? That wouldn't be good news.

But Jenny smiles and tells me, "We're not
too worried yet. There's a good reason she
might have gone into hiding."

And I find out the reason for her
disappearance later that week. I'm sitting
with my camera watching the lodge when
suddenly Gracie swims out of the tunnel with
something in her paws. It squirms as she
swims. Then she sets it down on the muddy
bank. It's so small and so cute. A tiny baby
beaver! It shakes itself and looks around while

Gracie dives back into the tunnel to bring out another and another. Three baby beavers.

Gracie fusses over them, washing them and pushing them further along the bank. I'm so busy watching that I almost forget to take photos.

But I do take photos. Lots of them. It seems impossible to believe these tiny baby beavers might one day hold the flood waters back. But I have to believe it. Because these little creatures are our future.

It feels extra special too. Because I'm the first to see the babies.

I look through the viewfinder and see the way the river has changed – the way it curls and loops and brings new life into this valley. I listen to the river singing its different song.

And it's only then that I notice the river that raged deep inside me has changed too.

CHAPTER 11

The beavers are so popular with visitors that our cafe is busy every day. As spring moves into summer, Emmi's mum and dad open up one of their fields as a campsite because people want to see the beavers at the nature reserve. People come from hundreds of miles away just to see them.

Mum had some of my wildlife photos printed and we sell them as cards in the cafe. The baby beaver photos have already sold out twice. Mum's even had to employ two people from the village to help serve and work in the kitchen. But Mum always does the baking – it's what she loves most.

I can't imagine living in the city again. It seems so long ago somehow. We've settled into the valley now. We're folded into the curves of its landscape. This place has become our home.

Mum seems happy, really happy. She laughs and hums as she works. She has found friends too in this deep river valley. She's made a life for us here. But there are times I see Mum staring out at the river. I know what she's thinking. Does the river still have the power to flood again and take away our dreams?

*

Summer turns to the first chills of autumn and I'm uneasy inside. It's not starting at secondary school that I'm so worried about. It's the memories of the storm from last year. Have the beavers had enough time to build

dams that will protect us? I hope we don't get any big storms again this year.

But the day before school starts, the weatherman shows a big swirling pattern of rain. I feel sick inside. It's happening again.

We don't open the cafe. We spend all morning carrying everything we can upstairs. We even take the tables and chairs into our bedrooms. I carry up all our pots and pans and teacups and saucers and plates and cutlery.

We move anything that isn't fixed to the ground. But Mum and I both know that if there's another flood, we'll be ruined. Mum won't be able to afford the repairs to the electrics again and we don't have the money to replace the oven and repair damaged floors and walls.

We pile sandbags by the doors to try to stop water coming in. But if it floods badly, we know sandbags won't protect us.

*

In the evening Mum and I climb the stairs as the rain begins to fall.

It rains and rains.

And rains.

Mum has switched the electricity off. We light candles instead, but they somehow make the dark seem even darker and the storm outside sound even wilder.

"Try to get some sleep," says Mum.

I climb into bed fully dressed in case I need to get up in the night. I go to sleep hoping that maybe this storm won't be as bad as last year.

But I'm woken by the wind. It rattles the loose gutter on the roof and sounds like a dragon climbing over our cottage. Rain hammers on the window.

I cross the room and fling the window open wide. I have to know what the river is telling me.

So much has changed and the river has learned to sing a different song.

It's a song that hasn't been sung for over four hundred years.

It's a wild song.

An ancient song.

A song that could be strong enough to hold the flood waters back.

CHAPTER 12

I'm still awake when there's a flash of lighting.
It lights the whole garden in neon yellow.

And in that split second, I see the river. It's
a wild monster surging along the bottom of our
garden. It heaves and twists and turns.

It roars.

"Mum!" I scream.

Mum is by my side and we look out into the
darkness.

There's another flash of lightning and I
see the river flowing up above the riverbank.

It slides towards us across the garden in a sheet of black water. The river hits the house and rises up the outside wall. I've never seen water rise so fast.

Mum holds me tight. "Oh, Cari!"

The water rises.

And rises.

But as fast as the water rose, it suddenly slips away, returning between the riverbanks. Mum and I stand in stunned silence. There is silence outside too. The rain has stopped and there is a break in the wind.

"It's over," I whisper.

Mum nods. She picks up a candle and walks to the top of the stairs. I don't want to know if

the flood has come into the house again. But Mum walks down, holding the candle high.

I hear her take a gasp of breath.

"Is it bad?" I say.

"Come down, Cari," says Mum.

I walk down the stairs and peer around her.

My eyes open wide. A small puddle has leaked in under the door, but that's all. Otherwise, the floor is dry.

Our dream, our home, has been saved.

*

When we get up the next morning, I hear people in the garden below. Jenny and Luke have come to check we are OK and move the sandbags away.

I go down to join them.

Jenny is grinning at me. "The beavers did their job," she says. "They've been working hard. I'm surprised they've had such a big effect so quickly. Usually it takes a couple of years to really slow the river."

"But there was a flood," I say. "It came up and went down really fast."

Luke nods. "The big dam the beavers made suddenly burst. That must have been why the water surged like that. But all the other pools held so much water back."

"There's no flooding in town either," said Jenny. "Apart from the pub car park, but everyone had removed their cars, so there's no damage."

"Are the beavers OK?" I ask. I'm suddenly worried if they got washed away by all the rain.

Luke smiles. "They're fine," he tells me. "You'll have to come up later and bring your camera. The beaver babies are having fun in all the new pools the rain has made."

We watch the news. The weatherman says there's good weather on the way, but he shows pictures of bad flooding in other valleys near us.

"The beavers saved us," I say.

"And you helped save the beavers," says Mum.

"Dad helped too," I say.

Mum smiles. "Why do you say that?" she asks.

I wrap my arm around Mum. "He showed me there are other ways to see."

"He'd be proud of us," says Mum. "You and me."

I take Mum up to the nature reserve to my favourite place and we sit in the shelter of some willow trees.

"It's so different to before, isn't it?" says Mum.

I nod. The beavers have made so many dams and pools, holding back the river. "Here they come," I say.

The beaver babies are so much bigger now, but they still follow Gracie around. They twist and tumble and play in the water. Maybe one day there will be more beavers in this valley, and in all the valleys around here.

I lift the camera to my eye as a beaver baby steps out onto the muddy bank.

I zoom in on its face and click the shutter.

I show Mum. "It's smiling," she says.

I look at the photo too. The baby's face fills the screen. I'm not sure beavers can smile, but it does look like it's grinning at the camera, with chubby cheeks and an upturned mouth.

And I smile too. Because I realise I'm happy. I'm really, really happy.

A breeze sighs through the willow trees and I hear a buzzard's cry from high above.

I listen to the river's song, to the gurgle and splash of water tumbling between the beaver pools. I can't hear the undercurrents or feel

the river raging deep inside me any more. I too have changed, like the river.

And I know it's OK to feel happy, even though Dad's not here.

I try to imagine Dad's face again. I don't want to remember him in hospital. I try to imagine the shape of him. We don't have many photos of Dad. He was always the one behind the camera.

But he was the one who taught me to see things differently.

I know he loved me.

And that's how I'll always think of him – my dad, behind the camera, smiling.

Our books are tested
for children and young people by
children and young people.

Thanks to everyone who consulted on
a manuscript for their time and effort in
helping us to make our books better
for our readers.